Little Tommie's Four B's

Written By Tommie Mabry

WestBow Press books may be ordered through booksellers or by contacting:

WestBow Press
A Division of Thomas Nelson & Zondervan
1663 Liberty Drive
Bloomington, IN 47403
www.westbowpress.com
1 (866) 928-1240

ISBN: 978-1-9736-4992-2 (sc)
ISBN: 978-1-9736-4993-9 (e)

Library of Congress Control Number: 2018915268

Print information available on the last page.

WestBow Press rev. date: 1/29/2019

Tommie
We Can Do It

If Tommie Can Do It,
We Can Do It
Written by Tommie Mabry
Illustrated by Eric Paige

Little Tommie's Four B's

This race is too long and hard.
I will never finish it.

Be Confident

Believe in yourself!
You can do this!

Ok, I can do this. I have to believe I can!
If Tommie Can Do It, We Can Do It

I still have a long way to go!

QUICKSAND

Be Determined

Do not quit, no matter how hard it gets.
Keep pushing!

START
Ok I will keep going.
QUICKSAND
FINISH

I’m almost there. I can see the finish line!

FINISH
2
1
3

Be Motivated

You will be proud of yourself when you're finished.

Ok, I will push myself
a little harder.

Yes I did it.

Tommie
We Can Do It

Be yourself

The person that you are is good enough!

I knew I could do it.
I am awesome,
And so are you.

ommie Can Do It,
Can Do It
Written by Tommie Mabry
Illustrated by Eric Paige

Printed in the USA
CPSIA information can be obtained
at www.ICGtesting.com
LVHW060351150923
758255LV00020B/204